What Do You Say?

First published in Great Britain by HarperCollins Children's Books in 2002
First published in paperback in 2010

1 3 5 7 9 10 8 6 4 2

ISBN: 978-0-00-664778-2

HarperCollins Children's Books is a division of HarperCollins Publishers Ltd.

Text and illustrations copyright © Mandy Stanley 2002

The author/illustrator asserts the moral right to be identified as the author/illustrator of the work.

The HarperCollins website address is: www.harpercollins.co.uk

Printed in China

What Do You Say?

BY MANDY STANLEY

ZZZZZZZZZZ

HarperCollins *Children's Books*

What do you say to a bee?

buzzzzzzz

What do you say to a dog?

woof

woof

woof

What do you say to a sheep?

baaaaa

What do you say to a duck?

quack

quack

What do you say to a cat?

What do you say to a mouse?

What do you say to a donkey?

hee haw

What do you say to a snake?

hissssssssssss

What do you say to a cow?

mooooooo

What do you say to a pig?

oink **oink**

What do you say to a LION?

rrrrr o o o o

roar...

And what do you say

to a little fish?

Hello little fish!

What do YOU say?

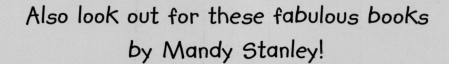

Also look out for these fabulous books by Mandy Stanley!

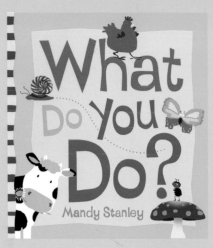

Paperback: 978-0-00-735353-8
Board book: 978-0-00-716579-7

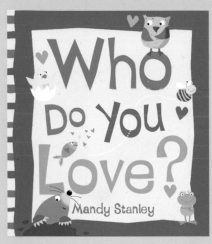

Paperback: 978-0-00-718406-4
Mini HB: 978-0-00-729342-1

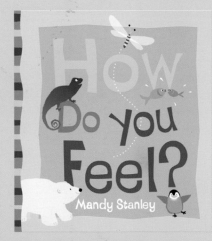

Board Book: 978-0-00-716578-0

Winner of
the Booktrust
Early Years
Baby Book
Award 2006